KT-133-312

Gallery Books
Editor: Peter Fallon

WAYS OF FALLING

Peter Sirr

WAYS
OF
FALLING

Gallery Books

Ways of Falling
is first published
simultaneously in paperback
and in a clothbound edition
in October 1991.

The Gallery Press
Loughcrew
Oldcastle
County Meath
Ireland

*All rights reserved. For permission
to reprint or broadcast these poems,
write to The Gallery Press.*

© Peter Sirr 1991

ISBN 1 85235 073 3 (*paperback*)
    1 85235 074 1 (*clothbound*)

The Gallery Press receives financial assistance from An Chomhairle
Ealaíon / The Arts Council, Ireland.

Contents

Acknowledgements

Acknowledgements are due to the editors of *The Irish Times*, *Ploughshares* (Massachusetts), *Poetry Ireland Review*, *Poetry Review* (London), *Quarry* (Canada), *Rhinoceros* and *32 Counties* (London, Secker and Warburg) in which some of these poems, or versions of them, were published first. The author acknowledges also the assistance of a bursary from The Arts Council / An Chomhairle Ealaíon in 1988 which helped get this collection under way.

Note

page 15   *vu' cumprà?* is a corruption of the Italian *vuoi comprarè?* (do you want to buy?). In Italy North African street vendors are sometimes disparagingly referred to as *i vu' cumprà*, from their supposed mispronunciation of this phrase.

An Exile

Old rivalries I bring you, news
of successes, failures, how *X* slights *Y*
and gets away, how the stones applaud
and the glasses shriek in bars —
not that you really want to know,
not that any of it matters, my stories
already yellowed with age, a bundle of letters
sent a long time ago, before I was born.
Whoever comes to see you comes like this,
a conversation left unopened on the table:
we have nothing really to say to you,
nothing to give you but the careless gift
of ourselves. Your eyes have no need
to meet ours, they sink inside
to the streets and squares, as they were,
to the young man
basking in the lamplight and listing, again,
what the city lacks. We watch you
leave again, traipsing grandly to the dock,
your future coming always oddly back
to this, one foot forever
on the gangplank. Now it's almost time to go
you fix us with your famous gaze and we know
our faces give you back as tribute
yourself, smiling, proud, your life
an open razor on the city's throat.

Rage's Heaven

Here's a wilderness, a petulance
of flung rocks, of trees knotted
and turned in on themselves, the sky low, sulky,
holding its face in its hands,
and the latest entrant
still seething and spluttering, washed up
on the tide of his own anger.
More behind him, fisting the surf, teeth clenched
or biting the wood that brings them in.
Daily they come, without end,
clawing the unreasonable air.
We meet them on the beach, requite
their passion with a snarl, we curse them
and knock them down then drag them screaming
to our cities, our frowning
dismantled kingdoms. God
but everything is rotten there!
The foul air rent
for all time with cries.
In our factories and studios their slavery begins.
Artisans of pure rage, they perfect
their craft, turning out
the broken crockery, the smashed mirrors
our wealth is built on, our good name.
All day, all night the thunder of the wrecking balls,
the tantrum bombs and the bullets whingeing, whingeing . . . .
All night, all day
in the flaring weather the towns
collapse, the sea invades,
and the rivers run riot. Already
the room I write this in
has had enough, the table trembles
under the page, the chair begins to rise
and the window turns blue then green then blue again
and spits itself to kingdom come.

From the Archives

They raise their hands to greet us
again, the dark kindred
undead of the video archives,
confident the light will hold
and their voices be heard, sure
that in its darkened room the future
will sit spellbound, regarding them
with the same lost eagerness
they use to tell their lives.
This one stands
awkwardly in a garden, on lurid grass,
speaking his name; he wears a smile
like a borrowed suit. Bored, we watch
the dog that pants beside him, the flutter
of his extinct shrubs, and ponder
the strange patterns of his clothes,
imagining their texture . . . yet one thing
saves him: a few seconds, about
halfway through when he stops, looks
harder at the camera and hesitates
then looks away,
tugs at his bright plaid shirt
and tugs again, enough to tear it.
This is all there is: nothing else
happens. He goes on with his story
just like the others, telling exactly
the same careful lies, eyeing us
with unconcern. Yet perversely we return
to that one gesture, the man helpless
in his garden, forgetting to go on,
as if he has just remembered
this will be remembered,
and suddenly willing his life to rise
to the trick that preserves it
reaches for something to give us,

something small and secret, something simple
slipped in among the bulky luggage
and getting here when the rest has strayed:
his own eyes that wander off
like tourists from the impressive scene
and coming back
not only find the place has gone
but the light itself has somehow
leaned too far and fallen down.

From the Brochure

Saint's ghost in a small church, lapped
by candles and the prayers of the faithful,

festivals of fire and food and the ghostly
immigrant faces, jewellery on a rug,

a row of watches, a mop and a bucket,
at the intersection a clamour of hands

on a windscreen, not work exactly
nor beggary either, but an old poverty

meeting the city halfway. Some give
and some pass with a curse, the dirt on their windows

after all the city's gift, with the fouled-up air,
the burgled furs . . . . In spite of ourselves

we live here, we collide
in the oddest places, in the heat that seeps

from a basement furnace, getting cooler by the floor,
in the all-night childish gurgle

of the plumbing and the watered-down
lives of the neighbours, we're drifting, coming together

on our dark lake, fingertips and toes
touching the sky that long since

clutched its belly and began to fall
bleeding fog onto the streets, falling softly

through the overhead wires, drowning
historic villas, tobacconists, the tenor

reaching out his arms to her, the audience in uproar
and the spiky cathedral bristling in its square.

Antique Lands

True, it is unbeautiful. But true too
I still dream it and often awake
I let it lie in my mind
some way back and as though glimpsed
idly from a passing craft. It has
its ways: coming quietly alive,
minding its own business, sometimes
bursting in to talk to me
in its boy's voice, making small boasts
I smile at, let pass.

This is how I hold it, and it holds me.
Something here must smile at this,
something polite in Tuscany, the sun
for instance low on the hills, about
to be gulped down. A good wine,
a good year, the elements agree.
I am walking round in circles here,
the way the path goes, on the red walls
of Lucca. At my feet the upper storeys,
roof gardens, balconies I almost reach.

The town snug inside its wall, packed tight
as the fruit inside its skin.
The night drops its ancient history,
the fruit darkens. And now the lovers come
to do their rounds, the joggers
having given up. They all pass quickly —
I am wearing the wrong leisurewear
and have come too far for the hands held
and the slow desire, bringing no gifts but the obvious
need, my mangled, smiling *vu' cumprà*?

Packing

She sees us but isn't interested
though she must know we watch her
too closely, that as she stands there

we have taken her body, folded it, and laid it flat
on piles of light, on the hard ground and the stones;
crush of sand and islands and the rich

ocean's cloak. How easy it is
and how good we are at it. The way,
holding the sky's ends between our fingers,

we walk towards each other
and work it to a neat blue square.
The sympathy! The breadth! O flash

geographies of the mind, and the heart pegged
to the eye's wire, about to fill up.
It is all us, snapped shut

and locked: the wind that drenches her housecoat,
that takes her startled sheets and plunges them
headfirst into the light.

Holiday Planet

Towers rising from a stony mist,
the planet trembling in its dust.
Hour after hour of leisure —
this after all the season we had sweated for,
coming with the others to see

the black breath of an autumn sky,
the white cage of a sunlit temple,
villages the wind had broken, ribs
of stone, paths streaming down
the endless mountain,

laid here that we might know
what poverty we came from, what desire
for somewhere essential to go
plus the scenery, trees placed to haunt us,
flowers everywhere on the ground

like blood spilled from a bright god
into whose heart they have plunged the light,
making the day all wound, making the night
come sirening down, to lift the body up
and bear it away . . .

The Names of the Houses

The village licks its fingers, belches, sighs, invites the yarn,
the childhood folly dragged up again and again
and as funny as ever. You know the pie has succeeded
in *Rustic Delight* while over in *Well-Satisfied*
the prospective son-in-law has them eating out of his hand.
Architecture of content, profit all year round,
and the houses full of mirrors. And all looked down upon
by the bloated in heaven, the sated
belt-loosening forebears telling it like it was,
joy without end, flagrant happiness
with, maybe, in the off-limits backstreet, the
    smelling-to-high-heaven
shithole hovel of the village weirdo —
look at him now, the witless fool, slopping out
in *The Place of Violence*, *The Maiden's Ruin*, the *Life as
    Normal*.

Two Masteries

1. *Proofs*

You know how it goes,
a myth of foolishness and greed,
clever, ironic Bacchus and the ass-eared
simpleton king cracking his teeth on gold.

Life is more complex than this.
I had money, finery, the usual
intrigues, mostly peace.
Gold!

Bacchus was a bore
like the rest of them; it was air I made,
not gold. I wanted things to fight back
the random pressure of my finger,

I wanted to thumb
some incredible wound. Instead
I watched everything I owned
shift gladly, *ping* into the light

with such simplicity it was hardly worth the fuss.
If I could have touched the sun
that too would have gone.
The light stayed, firm and believable

and with more space now to play in
which it seemed to like. My laces
were the first to go, then clothes,
bits of hair, and so it went on:

touch by touch the kingdom diminished,
gapped statuary and vanished arguments,
a lover tenderly disfigured.
I was a plague, an army, a breezy

philosophy proving its truths
in emptying rooms, how nothing
is much missed,
how the earth avoids us.

Eventually, I suppose, the gift failed
or the light got bored
and things came through again
palaces and houses, the art of the region

men with horses, swords, cries
I remembered. I have stayed here
like a ghost in training, managing
the occasional eeriness

among rocks and trees, holding things back:
that lost toy
always looked for, that body loosed to air
under your finger . . . .

2. A Bequest

         . . . whatever touches
then disappears, whatever hurts to linger
but sinks back, withheld:
a chisel lodged in silence, tapping away,
the leaves ambitious
on the trees that have launched them
and weary of their clamour will let them go,
masteries not only of the forgotten
but of the undone, failures not only
of the blessed hands to come down
but of the imagination to begin . . . .
                        I wanted
heavens unguessed at, burning to come through,
and go with what he might have given:
something disturbed and broken,
a voice crippled on its own hunger, a grammar askew.

Nostalgias

Attics webbed with yearning,
darkness desultorily plundered
by the light from a tiny window
like a cake with a piece missing.
Heavy and stale it waits, you wait
contemplating each other. Musty
dramas of revelation:
carefully you open the trunk, which creaks
and breathes dust on your arms, the first
confidence. Can you bear what follows?
The ribboned bundles? The dog-eared folders?
Someone's library of desire, the junk
of generations, still hopeful. One step at a time
you're returning. Unchanged,
unchangeable it waits, the final
threadbare flight, the familiar door,
the trunk open and the dust
scattering exactly as before
and the hands the same too,
exploratory, a pale inspectorate
converging on your clothes, your eyes,
your ribs they hold
one by one to the light . . . .

Diversion

The little airport's unfinished
to which the fog has sent us —
the terminal roofless, gaping,
the staff taken by surprise
yet greeting us with practised calm;
eagerly our luggage bulges in
on the single belt, as if it too
is anxious to impress, and in minutes
we're outside, waving to the small crowd
that's come to see us. *Passengers*
they seem to smile, *arriving here.*
The town itself is incomplete
and struggling to believe
its own streets, its hypermarkets
sucking in the light, its peacock
pumps preening in the forecourts
with not a car in sight.
The wind on our faces is warm —
like everything here, winter
has missed its deadline
but functions anyway.
Cheap cold, subcontracted frost,
cracks appearing in the sky.

A diversion, something maybe
to amuse you in the heart
of your pristine season, yet this is a place
I repeatedly visit, taking
whoever will come and dragging them
down the ragged paths of the region,
a leading citizen appointed to please,
who knows the place is not perfect
yet goes on pointing everything out,
the eyesore park, gouged
out of an old slum, where it festers,

greedy with green, and flashes
the cheap jewellery
of its ponds and fountains . . .
or like a prince let loose
on his father's kingdom and finding it
hardly exists — the royal forest
a few skinny conifers
nervous in the wind, the fabled capital
two skyscrapers and a brothel —
takes joyfully to the hills, emerging
years later as architect,
woodsman, prophet, breathless
with plans, spelling out
to whoever will listen cathedrals
and trees, the deep river that runs
surprising towns
the whole length of the country . . . .

Nothing is ever done
and what we love is not the journey
but making up the ground we walk on.
I think of our Sunday treks
to the woods outside our city,
marching with manic speed
through the drizzle and the mud
impatient with the view,
the smoky city and its bay,
the pines and firs like ourselves
hesitating on the hills, wondering
what more there was, a brightness
spread against the light, the houses and spires
lifted up and set down shining,
till we invented what we needed,
adjusting the picture
till it fitted whatever story

we were telling each other, beginning
when my father shut the front door
and we stepped into the car
to be taken god knows where . . . .

Is it any different now? The bus takes us
past the warehouses and factories
of the industrial heartland, back
towards a city we can barely see,
which nonetheless I send you,
its whoosh of traffic, its trams
all but invisible
like beasts in the fog, all
thunder and clatter, and brief
blue fire, and somewhere there, floating free,
the street I live in now, my eye
adrift already . . . .

Party Ode

Things are hotting up in the bright room. The sun
slumps gaily on the floor, enormously pleased with itself.
Your friends greet you, they tell you the latest
but it's beyond words at this stage, the language
has passed out, leaving only
the noises of extreme happiness, that carry so much farther.
The air is a glass perpetually breaking
into many thousand pieces. They cover your hair,
they fall on your face and all over your clothes.
For months after you'll be putting your hands in your pockets
and coming on the shards, your fingers will bleed with pleasure
but now someone hands you a drink, it adorns your hand
like a seal of office
and robed with smiles you walk through your kingdom.
Who cares
about tomorrow? Who can grieve
for the sour rage of tobacco, the tainted carpet,
the light raining on the distraught bottles
and the angry mob, driven beyond endurance,
marching all over the city, and converging on our heads?

Les Beaux Jours

Hell, we thought then, was the Hellfire Club
on a Sunday, our own perpetual
failure to ignite on top of a hill
put there to be driven out to on the wet
afternoons where our adolescence takes place;

the piss-stinking shack not the mad resort
of drinkers, gamblers, whoremongering
sons of the rich in velvet, desiccated fops
burning their calling cards on the fire,
beseeching the devil please to appear

because it's wet outside and all the other options
have long since expired — not this, but much worse
erected by a committee of parents
on a damp Sunday, to be stumbled up to
and slithered down from time after time

while your life fell around the place in stitches
wondering when you'd ever get round to it
and happy meanwhile to watch you
descend greyly into the carpark and count
the *Sunday Independents* spread out on the steering wheels,

raindrop after bloated raindrop slump onto the windscreen.

Escape Manual

There is always a way, surprisingly.
There is always some way to surprise
even this beady eye
open all decade and still a long way
from blinking. It is a world, or rather
it thinks it is *the* world, though it migrates farther
every day, higher up
into the black spaces, from where it stares
at its own sweet contour. O self-regarding
satellite, betray for once your orbit
and fall freely down, allowing
there is after all a way of falling,
there is always some way down.

Destinations

1

Something outside is ablaze with surprise.
The sun comes through
with a hungry clarity, taking its own.
The desk, and everything on it
rise to the light, as if they were dawning
on some quick mind, that holds them now
in wonder: lost things, beginnings, after all this time
discovered. Nothing here is mine. My own hands
lighten, as in a joy of recognition,
freed at last from the silent room, from their dark life.
The next one has already begun . . . .

2

Friends in their far rooms, the dead
in their endless homes,
streets that wander in the blood, addresses
still familiar, and those
hardly remembered, lives
held, relinquished . . .

3

Neither loved nor known, barely imagined:
a somehow friendly silence,
a place blank but hospitable, a body yearned for
but neutral: letter after letter comes, is scanned,
discarded, touch after touch arrives and is dissolved.

4

A landscape intent or convalescent:
everything there
is foretaste, echo, a tremor of entrance,
a still warm absence. It is the childhood of gods
or their ancient boredom. Here I come
in the small hours to explore, my hands empty,
my mind sucked dry: there is not only
nothing to say, there is nowhere to send it.
Yet here also I stay, invented by the air
and growing into it, each day
a little more securely: the first of my kind
amazed by my life, that lingers, and is spacious.

Swing

For all I know you're there
sitting quietly on the fallen willow

whose crushed branches have crushed the grass
listening to the last noises of the garden

that might be an elegy for the old tree.
They left the swing there, its worn rope

laps the branches, its seat half sunk
in leaves and earth, and for all I know

you have taken the light in your hands
and gripping it with all your strength

are swinging towards me, away from me,
moving all the time nearer and farther

until the beginning and the end are the same,
until you have become

a faint shudder in the darkening canopy,
the shadows swaying all around me.

You

You do not exist, nonetheless
your house glitters on its severe coast
and the landscape is full of rocks

as the houses are full of people
who know you, who, if summoned,
would remember how you came there,

what you wore, the colour of your hair.
Nothing is empty there and nothing
goes without notice though there is a silence

you won't touch, loving the journey
between the end of words and the beginning
of the world. You let the house drift,

the rocks float and the sea forget,
you let the sun sink on its grate
spilling ash on the planets,

then almost with reluctance, almost as if
it might have been possible to linger there,
you bring them back,

you let the darkness unclench its fist
and the careless breath
scatter us in the light.

Here and There: A Notebook

A house overlooking the sea,
your spirit-rinsing view —
my house   here.
I can feel the whole page soar,
I can peer through the earth
down
to the solid foundations
of your letters, your poems.
I stand
in stupefaction outside, out of sight,
listening to the wind
tear up the bay, the waves say *this*
is it. Smoke from your chimney
haunts the air briefly
then disappears . . . .
In the evenings there is the radio,
erratic symphonies
braving the storms, the mountains,
conversations
distance makes important
and interruption, the world
an alien glamour, a signal
unreliable yet surprising.
Lifelines!
When you switch on the light
the hedges are astounded,
the dark tide
ebbs from your window, a neighbour
comes to call, a silence broken by small news,
the whiskey pouring   Oh plodder's
pastoral   Yet forgive me.
It's late here
where I sit hunting
authenticating details,
fleshing out that stretch of sea

till it washes up to my own door,
polishing stars while the sky
deepens and the street subsides
and suddenly
everything is stone walls and telegraph poles,
placenames and elaborate fauna
yielding one by one
secrets that keep me here.

を ぞ

Here is a tight terrace
through whose thin walls
lives leak continually,
laughter and rows,
howl of petulant dogs,
my neighbour's piano
spilling daily into my head.
The street is narrow, the houses
so close to glance out the window
is always to be met by eyes
glancing back. Humane horizons . . .
A Turkish family
lives opposite, the men serious
and dark suited, the women in their
flowered dresses and headscarves.
How many generations?
How many children are there?
What is she thinking about,
the woman whose eye I catch,
smoking a cigarette by the window,
her elbow resting on the sill?
The men sit in bars so bare, so ugly
the natives hurry past, wondering at
that plantless brightness,

kitchen chairs on a wooden floor, a din
of maleness — strange islands
in a sea
of *Gemütlichkeit*.
What do I know?
I've lived here a year
hermetically sealed
from the life of the street,
worrying about connections.
Yesterday, a week to Christmas,
a man I've never seen before
called with branches of catkin,
told me to put them in water,
then disappeared.
Last year, on New Year's Eve, at midnight
I stepped outside to watch
the fireworks. A door opened
across the street, the house
whose curtains are always drawn,
and a man came out, unshaven,
wearing an old string vest.
In his hand he held a revolver
which he fired twice into the air,
then he came and shook my hand
and went back in, smoke trailing
from the gun barrel.
His son keeps his Alfa Romeo
outside my window, sleek and black,
on the bonnet a huge transfer
of a wolf snarling. The man himself's
tattooed, forearms aglow
with sex and power.
I prick my skin
to let the pigment in
but little holds.

Again and again
the eye migrates, complains,
wherever it goes
is a city like this
undiscoverable,
in the dim suburbs of perception
a surfeit of detail.

ॐ ॐ

I keep your letters in my pocket,
your flowers, your silences.
I carry your life around with me
as a comforting fiction,
a *dinnseanchas*
rooting me to the spot, the notion
that we may yet belong,
that the fields and the cities are veils
we may yet lift, running our fingers
along the fabulous skin,
that the world may yet reach us
as a kind of tenderness,
holding us in its grip,
that the fingers don't open
and the arms fall slack
and our bodies stand
desolated there
where the very air is loss.

Newtown Road

1

A notebook full of remembered trees
A playroom filled with resurrected toys

The city reduces itself to a single street
The street to a single house

Grey stone green door paint peeling
From the railings, blackening my hands

The house tries hard to complete itself
Rooms come clear, falter, vanish

Stairs spread out like anecdotes
In wandering minds, searching for a conclusion.
  Surely . . .

A door swings open, closes again
Slowly the house leans out, slowly

Collects the garden, reaching down
To the crushed lawn, a high stone wall

Reaching even the apple trees
In the orchard at the bottom, out of bounds,

The rickety willow
Like an old umbrella

Reaching down to me too
Playing late with Chiko

The landlord's browneyed brownthighed niece
From Canada, before we collapse on the grass

Exhausted, but determined to stay
As long as we can like this

Trespassing, watching the night, the stars ripening
On their dark branches.

2

Stashed in the garden
With my notebook and binoculars

I case the house, observing
Its comings and goings, its show of lights,

Its careless treasures
No one remembers.

I have come here for this.
I have shinnied up the long black pipe

And gently, not a sound, lifted
The kitchen window, eased

The door, a crack, a hairline fracture
In which my father lights

One of the five cigarettes
He allows himself, and my mother

Has poured them both a drink.
It is late, the children are asleep,

No one else is here.
I have come back for this,

I come here every night
Holding a mike to the thread of light

In which my parents live.
Ten years of conversation,

Of smoke rings and silences,
Tenderness and argument,

Of watching TV, or doing nothing,
Of scattering the evidence,

I creep around in the small hours
To assemble, pilfering

A packet of Sweet Afton,
A ball of wool, handkerchiefs

And hairpins, a postcard
From Tramore, a corner

Of the *News and Star* — everything held and relished
Before I stuff it in my bag.

Ten years they live here, blow-ins
In the tight city

Of my childhood. Signposts,
Street names, the house collapsing

And rising again, up and down
Until there's left

A single brick, a stone crumb, a smudge of dust
Staining a fingertip, enough still

For a thin shout. This is it.
This is what I came here for.

Cinemas

Put it this way, the world that unfolds
outside the obsessive window is the window's own,
a short feature on an aspect of an aspect
of a portion of the larger view, and though you lean
towards *the world* or *we*, nobody's fooled.
Everything you see is the poignant entry
in the film festival, the one from the country
whose name you would like to be able to pronounce
though garbling its syllables is itself a kind
of faith, one part flattery, one part rebuke.
When it comes you rise to cheer it, pushing
the big budgets from your brain, the names of stars
too like us, and everybody's dreams. The camera
   catches
a simple light, faces turn towards the darkness,
looking directly at you. Image succeeds image
and it is difficult, like following the argument
of a tangled poem, which, you sense,
is coming close, but slowly and with some pain
stumbling behind its torch of instinct, intuition —
all those precarious fires we carry round,
veering towards an Olympics of desire, in which no
   one
knows the rules but everyone has ideas, revelations,
   blinding
flashes of what the thing is and who the winners are.

Wires

An old man in green overalls, painting the pigeon coop
that takes up a good third of the tiny garden.
He's always there, tending and improving, always
in green overalls and boots, miraculously busy.
Sometimes his wife joins him, brings him tea
and stays to chat a little before going back inside.
Mostly it's just him and a tired old cat
tied by a long wire to the washing-line — he's spent
all his life like that, five square metres of grass
to patrol, up and down the length of the line
like a tram. These days he hardly moves, just sits
all day in the same spot, very occasionally, and with
a heaviness, a visible reluctance, as if he felt obliged
to prove his catness one more time, gets up and prowls,
looks a little fierce, challenging rooftops and hedges,
then goes back to his usual patch and stays there
watching the pigeons come shitting home
tugged by their invisible wires. Days like this
the whole sky seems pulled down around our heads
like a blanket we won't let go. An eternity yet
before the bright morning of the soul: meanwhile, the
     poem
circles above the suburbs, having lost its way,
desperate for a wire to tug it home.

Pumping

My old lives wake up. Excitedly
they dress, rush down into the kitchen
demanding food, attention. Cereal voices,
milky moustaches, telling me their dreams.

I sit back and listen to myself
riding round the block on the Eska Special
hardly believing my luck. Suddenly
the shine blurs, I can just make out the name

and *Made in Czechoslovakia*. Something else has changed:
the bike's powered by an invented engine —
strips of cardboard pegged to the spokes,
snagging the real. Who do I think I am?

Near the end of its life I took the saddle off
and found the pump. It had lain there
all that time undiscovered, its shine intact,
a secret heartbeat. It comes to me, oddly clear,

as if, never used, it ached now to connect,
blurting out air like the effort to remember,
a dead weight fed back to a phantom valve
and returning with its own breath . . . .

The One Dim Thing

See, how he has turned to her, to that one spot
where her neck takes the light and whitens
to perfection: see how his finger strives to enter
that light and how, again, it is the same room, the same

heartbreaking light, the light of argument and desire,
the one illumination here: obsession's heaven,
the one dim thing relentlessly reached for,
the single gesture failing infinitely to accomplish itself.

He gives it up and settles back, he looks out the window
at the grey town: spires and rooftops, his own life creeping
like a burglar there. They lie absolutely still, the end of love
seeps through them like a drug, and because they are different

it works differently in each. She is drowsy now, almost asleep,
but his sceptical hands start out again, on their
ancient journey. They are not his hands now, they stray from
    him
like innocents, pilgrims who left the very hour

the faith shifted. Soon he will leave or she will,
and his hands will come back to him, days later, or weeks,
in the final scene. Much has yet to be decided:
whose room, what town, what exact degree of passion, pain.

In the end nothing of this may remain,
neither the room nor them, not a limb, not a single hair —
though the light I capture is the light they've left
and every shot is bereft . . . .

Spools

He sits in a booth in the empty laboratory
and listens to the sound of the language
exciting itself. Wave after wave
of desire, words locked in their passionate grammar.
In there somewhere, the beautiful girl
he must carry off, stirring in an inner chamber
perhaps dreaming of him. Backwards, forwards
he juggles the tape. It has to be there,
the secret door, the one way through
to her smile of recognition and fear,
the gathering up of her perfect body,
then the long struggle home, the kiss
that wins her over. Troops scour the hillsides,
the king fumes. Epics of flight and discovery,
their legend printed on a hundred hollows,
the hearts of the people their refuge.
The tape runs and runs. He listens for a sigh,
a heartbeat, anything. He hears
the cunning voice of the storyteller
spellbind the future, winding it back to him
like a spool, into his ancient room
and back through centuries, to the first telling,
to the first stirring of the language itself
gathering the morning on its tongue
and trying to keep it there.

The Eros Touch

Only then did we realise
how generous love is,
stepping outside to bestow ourselves
on a grateful world, turning everything to praise.
The sun hymned down on the little street,
the pavement trembled beneath our feet.
Amazing, how little we had seen before,
how meanly we had looked. That new block of flats
for instance, hurrying up at the corner,
near the vegetable shop, the high crane hanging indulgently
over the town centre. And some sweet sadnesses,
healable: how we paused to mourn
the shabby Chinese departed forever.
(Why didn't we eat there more often!)
A Greek takeaway was in its place, blue and white,
imagining the sea, and out of sheer compassion
we fed on *giros*, *souvlaki* with double sauce.
Every day we passed we wished the business well
as if our livelihood depended on it, or our lives;
as if love were the new religion and this
its hasty, awkward temple.
And yet it wouldn't take, no one entered,
the Greek leaned on his painted counter
watching German television. We hurried past now
shy to catch his eye. A day we smiled
to see a sign chalked up outside
FREE WATCH WITH EVERY MEAL, and imagined
we'd stop time and re-invent it here,
taking the white wrists in our hands, clothing them
with the marvellous plastic and flashing digits.
But the business failed, they carried out
the Parthenon, Venus in a fishing net.

The kittenish world had stopped purring,
stopped arching its back on our laps
though we kept on stroking it,
nursing our bitten fingers
long into the night.

'Of the thousand ways to touch you . . . '

Of the thousand ways to touch you
I select this one
the finger running gently
from toe to thigh and back again
its route fixed, like a tram
snug beneath its wires
                              above
my finger now, bolt after bolt of blue fire
rocking the air . . . .

A Few Helpful Hints

Tell them what you like. Tell them
the world is flat and when you get to the edge you fall
into the usual darkness, hell if you like
but anywhere will do, any storied space
mythical returners have whined of, salty
and smelling of loss. Tell them the rain falls
and steals slyly up and falls, and falls —
tell them everything twice for emphasis
and then again the next day for revision.
Set them tests on the same thing time and time again.
Tell them most of life is repetitive
and this will stand them in good stead.
Tell them about gravity and love,
drop the whole world on their heads
if you have to, the broad curriculum
of hatred and desire and the need for money
and love, tell them some things are permissible
and some less so, though ideally we'd prefer it
if you left that to us. Above all
don't be heavyhanded, keep a light tone,
encourage them to laugh, encourage them to believe
they are getting away with something when they do.
Encourage them to see you as a fragile
merely human being. Forget things, mix up names
and be occasionally unfair in the allotment of marks.
Tell them about yourself if it helps. Allow your emotions
to enter the syllabus, when reading a poem, or telling them
things that have happened. Break down if you have to,
rail against the world and its mindless cruelties.
Tell them we could all be blown out of it
or the sun might go out or too much of it get through.
Tell them not to use aerosols, organise a project
on it. Projects are good. We like to stress
the need to work together. Harmony
is the oil in the machinery, or something

like that. Tell them about the men who came to save us
with beautiful voices and a poetry
we would like to have found time for, we may yet
retire to. Tell them about those
who have still to come, shuffling in awkwardness and anger
from the cardboard slums that tremble even now
on the outskirts, whose poems
may already be struggling in our blood
or hurtling through the dark cathedral spaces
achieved and pure, unsettling the stars.

Conquistador

Decked out in the complete Real Madrid strip
Francisco, our first foreigner, is scoring
goal after contemptuous goal
in the overgrown field.

Our house is too small for him,
the whole country lacks grandeur.
He curls the thin lip of his English
and pines for Spain.

Years later I surprise myself
at the same game, mocking the flat land
for its lack of mountains,
its surplus of water,

running rings round the natives.
In two years I haven't learned
how to be here
yet how pleased I am with myself

hunched in the shabby café
over a miniature beer, brandishing my life
like a pithy quotation, and dribbling effortlessly
from absence to absence . . . .

Perfection

That brilliant opening, those flashes of the something pure
one breath away from fire . . .
Sometimes we almost get there. Or you do. Your look tells me
    now
you are the real thing, beyond correction,
polished down to the last comma.
Everything fits. Everything progresses naturally.
The hair falls on your shoulder
as if all its life it had known it would get there
and rests now with all the confidence
of the true impulse. Line by line
your body takes fire, your image warms the room.
You are complete. I watch and shiver. There's nothing left
    to do
but seal yourself snugly in the brown envelope of your coat
to be slit open in another room by other hands
so astonished at what they find
all else ceases, all poetry holds its breath till you lie
printed on the sheet.

Back in the Attic

His plight is hopeless, my hands are tied.
I will hang him on the hour
in a botched noose from the banister
and leave him there to encourage the others
who, nevertheless, will recover his body
and bury him tenderly at the end of the garden,
in the flowerbed by the wall, the crowds weeping
to the Last Post on paper and comb.
And tonight he'll hear again
the grave voice of Attic Radio, *The appeal has failed*,
and listen for my slow feet on the wooden stair,
the brass handle loosening in my palm;
he'll refuse to see me when I lift the lid,
staring into space as if he didn't care.
I'm sorry, offering him a last cigarette, a letter home.
Nervously I take him out, I know
anything can happen now, my own hands
surprise me, cut through the wool with a stolen blade,
my body rage blindly on the floor, in a battle
it could take all evening to decide.
I have been killing him for years, with authentic cruelty
and disappointed fuss — the ludicrous way
his legs stick up when he falls, like a grown-up at play,
his bored endurance of the worst I can do.
He is too much a toy
with his stout elastic and trademark scar, too close
to the serious world whose gift he is, and to which
he has wholly returned.
I lift the lid to find the same
indifferent blue eyes stare through mine.
Fifteen years on death row! Gently, I take him out
and set him on the floor, both of us
inept and adult, sprawled in a corner, our hands tied,
waiting patiently for the fiendish executioner
to finish his tea and come upstairs.

The Reflexive Tradition

The house adrift,
the house idling in the heat, dreaming us,
dreaming the fantastic attic spaces,
dim childhood swimming
among the lost
avuncular furniture, opening boxes.

This one holds
the burst bubble of Christmas:
a spiky disarray, the shameless
colour-coded branches, the tripod stripped
of its cardboard skirt,

and this one, a tea-chest from Rangoon, selected hardbacks
from a literature of self-improvement
coming on pat to the amazed dark
Your Life in Your Own Hands
Ten Steps to Success

Here too the skilled assertive children
on their pure adventures
swimming off secret islands
the whole 'hols'.
My nine year old life pauses for reflection,
fingering the tradition. How do you continue?
How long can your own breath hold?

Movies

Meanwhile our parents had made it, they were old hands
slouching in the wine glow
of an endless dinner. Everything was authentic now
from the clothes worn to perfection
to the casual conviction of their voices
spilling out the open door. They were hitting their stride
and the house sat silent and absorbed,
watching, listening. Their lives were so well done
we are still struggling with our coats
in the threadbare plush,
still blinking at the lobby's air
of spent invitation,
pushing drugged limbs through a glass door
and disbelieving every step of the journey home.

At the Cultural Centre

The blond mannequin at the Flemish Cultural Centre
in the gold coat and gold tipped shoes
waiting for the fashion spectacular
smiles at an invisible mirror. A slim girl
shakes her gorgeous curls
and is beautiful. In a corner

the poets have gathered, talking
in the accent of their hard northern city.
Their clothes seem odd, out of place, their voices jar
like static on the erotic line
of Friday night in Amsterdam.

After the reading
in a small room of the cultural centre
of a small, divided nation,
in fierce darts of urban Scots
for a handful of ex-pats and a party of schoolgirls
who will be discussing this in class

there will be a *céilí* in the National Folklore Centre,
a short speech on Europe's
fascinating diversity.
The blond clicks his gilded toecaps.
The bar is crowded. The schoolgirls seem excited.

We go home with Glasgow,
singing in our ears, returning
to our own outskirts, the cold
provincial night, the still suburban street, the room
after room after room our lives invade,
building their empires
round the difficult dialects, the haiku heart
pouring itself out in the backwoods quiet.

Their Laughter

Anything can happen here, though it's dinner
and everybody seems calm, my father
winding himself down with jokes and sighs,
my mother smiling and eating. I shuffle them like cards
until something turns up, a house full of weapons
and strangers, a garden mined with quiet.
In love with death, I give them each
two minutes to live and leave the table.
I set the charge and wait for it, first
the explosion, then the indulgent shrapnel
piercing the hall and landing, raining on me
all the way up the stairs.

My Own Voice

I walk into the room, an average citizen
home from the mines, the office, the dim
labour of the fields, I allow myself to be greeted
by the friendly wooden shape, round and smooth.
Such importance to come home to!
I love the heavy way it squats on the table
and seems to draw the air down onto it.
I have taken the back off and put
my own recorded voice inside
but the voice that comes out is the radio's,
not mine: suave and serious, a voice to be listened to
with pleasure, surprise, a voice you can't refuse.
Sometimes it has grave things to tell and you feel
the attic hold its breath, awed by event.
The enemy is approaching, we must be strong.
Sometimes it's just for fun, or dryly amazed
at its own survival, it reports adventures
from the heart of travel, an old friend whose life
is addressed to you. Sometimes when the tape runs out
I let it all go on inside my head, continuing
to astonish the populace, silencing lives
across the country. And sometimes the imagination fails,
I freeze on air and the radio suddenly
becomes itself, old junk, its innards ripped out,
its big knobs and cloth grille on which
a broken girl reclines, playing the flute.
I would like to jump on it, smash it.
Or I look at it and wish
it would speak to me of its own accord,
crackle out of its silence some ancient song,
some old sponsored ghost —
I will it to be haunted by the voices
it gave freely to the air, or by those
it refused, the rejected scripts and failed tunes
sent out at last. But nothing happens.

I stare at it, helpless, I set the dial
to Stavanger, Hilversum, Limoges
but all of Europe has disappeared.
There are no ghosts left in the world
just the relentless silence of old radios.
My lives lope across the desert of the attic,
exhausted. They climb into my brain and immediately
are asleep. The game is obsolescing.
I hear noises from downstairs, then my father
coming up. He opens the door, he rips
the back off my brain and puts the tape inside,
then waits for me to do the same.
We stand there smiling, running for the umpteenth time
voices we pretend are ours.

The Sun Trap

Sitting there, in that same room,
she feels him come, not *from* anywhere
and not especially to her
but to his old life, to the room itself:
a kind of heaviness, as if his body
slunk again in the chrome chair
and watching television she could feel
the ache to focus, the picture
begin to blur, the sound hum meaninglessly
and over it all
the steady current of his pain

or sitting outside, on the patio
lifting her head to the sun
and feeling him enter as the pressure
behind her own eyes, feeling the air
tighten to a squint and her head
go slack as his, her body crumple in the light,
washed onto it, the island
full of everything, too late arrived at.

Through the Window

As if, sickening of the view, you only had to look
far enough out the window, past
the serious shapes of the rooftops, the spires,
and find, somewhere off-centre, the harmless suburb
where the days wait like bandages
and the nights are a sweet coolness
and all of childhood simply this, a convalescence;
a white room waking into the same few sounds:
water running softly, sleep-happy voices,
the radio lapping the floor as you dress.

As if some part of the mind must always give up
and look for a smaller place, a pension
of painless perfections. My father, for example,
is always healthy here, his body young and trim
and always *moving*. I hear his knees cracking on the stair
like muffled gunfire as he comes to call me:
I see him running backwards, arms up,
face serious, catching the ball I've thrown
to test him, his safe hands seeming to grip the future,
his energy like a current arriving at

his own helpless body a decade later,
charging it somehow, and flowing on into mine
as I lift him up and help him walk.
I am dragging the past, healing us,
the boy throwing the ball who doesn't ask
for this, the hands lost in the simple act
of catching. Year after year I arrive here,
out of breath, and stretch my hands into the air
as if *this* were the image, and they had turned to me,
Were you watching us? Did you see what we did?

The Guest

1. *To the New Arrival*

Welcome, whoever you are.
The door was open and in you came
as you had to. The door was open
and the street a pulsing breath
which had to bring you here.
I expected you, but nonetheless
am taken by surprise
as you must have been to find me
so unhinged, so lacking
in the usual resistance. Through
the long corridor and into
the right room, a breeze's
sudden confidence. Doubt will come later
with the rest, but for now
I'm glad you stirred and I stirred
enough to let you pass
through my open arms.

2. *At Sea*

Instead of a dialogue
that flurry of acquaintance
the troublesome business
of eyes and words
let us be content with distance

the underpraised, the awkward
and stubborn

I myself have spent so long
on the vocabulary of approach
wasted decades

on tender approximations
on the parts of the body
that must always be going somewhere
and so fêted the journey

that now I have no hunger
to embrace you, no bones
to give you, no desire
to travel towards your gaze,
                              blundering
late into the companionable port
but would celebrate the sea spilling miles around us yet
the night tossing its coins of light
and closing them in its careless fist.

3. *Songs*

I will reach it,
the truly
plangent note
                 welcome cries
of the self-host
crowding the room.

                 ❧ ❧

Today is a day for keeping out.

The intruding air, the white
presumption of light. Beware.
The room is well guarded.

                 ❧ ❧

It is very quiet.
Something must bite.

Patiently I sink the line
into a pool of concern
and wait. More quiet
                then
the hooked heart tugs
and comes pouring out.
It pulses coyly on my palm.
It is not afraid. It knows me.
Knows that cold as I am
it is safe there;
in that endless pool
nothing taken is too small
to be thrown back.

∾

A song comes in from the neighbour
unbidden but confident,
leaning out of its black box
as far as it can. Adventuresome

air, heartstain worn
on a sleeve of clarinet . . . .

The Weight

Let me stay

here in your arms, in my own arms
holding you. There is such weight

to be held. I am afraid
of the weightlessness of tomorrow

of the emptiness of hands

as if they had been created
for this one weight and can hold

no other . . . . The night
falls away, a heaviness

slipping through fingers of light
as we slip back into ourselves

taking our arms with us. But

though they go they are ours no longer,
they are so much slackness
                              adrift

in a light they do not fit,
they are the memory of weight.

The Pursuit

And if you were here there would be
that fury of touch, that drive to believe,
flesh raining on flesh till the whole
field flourished and I ached again
to bring you home. There would be
the usual fears and holdings back, the perpetual
sweated harvests borne uncertainly
yet also with joy. There would be
the high speed of language as we struggled to reach
the place where at last we could rest,
the pined for slow resort where the mind
brakes and the language sleeps and we had
nothing to do but linger in the interim.
Instead of which I send, and not even to you,
but to something inside my head, the expected
speculative lyric, the flashlamp scouring
the cave of love and finding a spider-spray
of voices, ancient tangles flirting in the beam.
I have resorted to an old trick,
hymning the distance again, hoping to have you come
very slowly from there to here, hoping at least
to have something come, that would be more
than this fruitless search for you
becoming the search for words for you
which are not you but where, for now,
you might be crouching, a fingertip, an eye, a hinted
exhalation on the air. Relentlessly I dream
of our arrival, a midpoint, some northern town
waking pristine in its dawn, and us there
anxious to begin, pursued by our old
offended selves, till we almost disappear,
living by hints, half things, tremblings,
blurred to each other in the retreating town,

in the fog that is our own breath
pulsed from fearful lungs, till finally
we've lost them — and become legendary —
the bill-posting, reward-offering, maddened
old ghost and all his underfed, regretful soldiery.

Mid-table

The wine on the table.
The fruit in its cracked bowl.
The hunched shoulders of your lover
as he leans over: his elbows
ruffle the blue check cloth;
with his right hand he tugs at his hair.
He is pulling from his chair

like . . . and here it begins again . . .
like a boat leaving the harbour,
not much of a boat, no sooner
imagined than broken, and pulling out
into a sea it has ill-prepared for.
The wine heaves and the fruit
shudders in its bowl. He is making waves

on the cloth, his elbows are storm gods
— why not? — stirring it up. He is moving
both towards you and away from you.
Your face has become
the frightening
sheer coast of an alien land
and he is lost

in mid-table, making a hames
of the navigation. Why
flounder like this? Why listen
to the mind in its caged ocean
sicken on its
drift of utterance? In the mess, the somehow
necessary fuss,

loss itself gets lost.
What we are left with
is the pictured lover

straining the furniture, and your
honest coast he will never reach.
What we are left with is the boat gone down
and the story drowned; an empty voice, a prettiness.

A Valediction

A difficult old age. The fastidious elegist
sat clutching his desk as if that too
would disappear. What little remained
he had already remembered, had already
forgotten and half recalled. Around him
the careful sadness of his study,
regarding him, the dust already shifting,
excited, wondering
how the thing might be done.

Death of a Travel Writer

Why have I not written?
But there is nothing here to write of.
No, there is too much here to write of
but it is not allowed. Besides
we have no system here for sending letters,
we survive on the bright spurt of our voices,
folded tightly in their envelopes of hurt,
their scented anguishes. What did you expect?
A monthly folio of flame? Descriptions of the landscape,
our bright-eyed local monsters, ourselves aching
in their damp regard? I wrote too many letters.
Is this why they sent me here? So much here.
Scene after scene visited upon the brain
but unusable. Cities weeping for their creation,
fields awash with a thousand dawns, watched by me
from window after window after window.
Suns, moons, things like stars
but brighter, harder, out of bounds . . .

A long time ago.
A dark, damp land.
A narrow room and the day
sloping sidelong in, light
as reluctant as ever.
Noises outside,
rough shouts of the populace,
water lapping the quay wall,
a rat or two, in a hurry.
Wondering how little of the place
I could afford to see
and still get done. The book as ever
overdue, the woman wanting her money.

Months of this,
of reading about the architecture
in rooms ever smaller,
of the country out there, wide
and explorable, things never seen,
fabled; lives unread yet.
I came to this place weary.
There had been too many like it.
It was time to stay inside
believing whatever I was told
or making it all up. I made
a narrative of cheap hotels
and hurried beds.
In the light from the harbour
I harboured odd ambitions.

First Ambition

To push through the cities
with the obstinate delicacy
of the blind tourist
who, in spite of you, knows his way,
who asks to be shown
everything, enjoys
your discomfiture. The cathedral, he says,
The Last Supper, the pigeons
anxious in the square.

Who will infinitely ignore
your blustering gifts:
the white stick, the faithful labrador,
the fumbled intersection
and the pavements raked

for pity. Who will touch nothing.
Who will give you back
his mythic fingers, his preternatural hearing
and go without memory or miracle

through the darkest streets.

More Impressions of the Forest

        O still
literature of motion.
I lift my eye
like a pen heavy with longing
and boredom. Days come like ledgers
I very slowly fill.

Inept, inadequate
vocabularies of inquisition.
The stars come out
asking question after question
until the eye gives up, confesses
everything, and melts without murmur
into the fire.

First Journey

What would it have been?
Sunlight, say, radiant
ceilings, some bright pool
burning the floor, that silently
or with little laughs I hymned . . . .

Wasn't it this I wanted,
want now? Some modest
magnificence, modestly sung
and by me alone:
                    the first thing seen,
the child adrift
on his ship of delight, without
paper or instruments . . . .

How I Died

In the jungle, savaged
by wild beasts I could not name.

A street in Sicily. July.
The air rent by soundless bullets.

In my room, yellowed with age,
absorbed by thick pillows, lies.

Rising, like steam, from
the fetid waters of my brain.

Floundering in the breasts
of a serving-girl in Flanders

Jakharta   Mombasa   Cefalù
Lübeck   Achill   Alba

A son in every port
lifting his hands in hate.

Some Necessary Languages

Atakama   Xwarsi   Yecacome
O Kamtchadal
Nawa Arči
and Kupeño   Kucarete
Puelce   Guenoa

Quapuči   Dido
Tomateka   Kakomo
and the quick darts of Matagalpa

Letter to Whomever

This one is smuggled out
by, if you like, a friendly
guard, or a poor one
needing the money to feed
wife, children, or some private need
of his own. It is written,
as you see, in haste
on brittle stuff that may not last
even long enough for you to read it,
in blood or the blood's ghost,
poor and thin, trying very hard
to scare up a voice, to say
something as it leans over the bed
almost comically. Stay
where you are. Don't stir.
Continue lying on your side,
face half sunk, a hand
thrust under the pillow
as if it might find something.

Me maybe. Take it. Read it
in your head, one word
at a time, coming like ads
in the movie of your sleep.
It may wake you: if so
let me apologise now and still
don't move, don't leave the bed
to hunt the cause, don't look
for my dim outline retreating
into curtains, clothes
slumped as always on the chair
and on the floor. I will
have long gone. I should
never have come, even
as these few words
on their brittle stuff
in blood or the blood's ghost.

Some Necessary Equipment

Sensible clothes; a robust character;
paper, pens; agility; lack of money;
a compass; a troubled childhood;
mosquito nets; anger; tinned pears;
ointments; a strong stomach;
a weak heart; a small typewriter;
credit cards; memories; good boots;
impressive gifts; words; a folding stool;
weapons; a curious sexuality;
binoculars; acne; a motionless adolescence;
whiskey; cigarettes; an inadequate body;
magazines; books; telephone numbers;
faith; cruelty; Van Houten's cocoa;
gas burners; matches.

How I Died

Boiled not in oil but in the pool
in which my face quivered for love.

On a bleak day in February,
of hunger and self-pity.

Borne aloft on tribal spears,
celebrated and enjoyed.

Knocked flat at the intersection
reading *Invisible Cities*.

Having discovered the lost empire.
Having discovered her

breasts   thighs   cunt   arse
toes   neck   and burnt my lips

in the pits of her arms. Of
loneliness and lack of sex.

Second Ambition

On a bright day, in the thick of it,
while chatting with the ambassador's wife
or making notes on the sacred axes
still upright in their groves, to vanish
without excuse or apology, having failed
to pack and neglected to leave a note;

a quick burst, spilling light and wine
but otherwise without fuss, leaving no mess
to clear, no mild griefs to be stirred
reluctantly on the appointed day;
and walk out the door, through the clearing,
through the solid, recorded trees

with eyes but no language, with hands
but no desire to make anything of them;
without desire; to be pure air
gusting from the sea, flooding the valleys
and wanting nothing but to go on like this,
travelling the earth as its own unthinking breath.

A Suburban Childhood

A table stained with spills, ruined.
Chairs, pictures, carpet the sun rifled,
leaving his mark. The heavy curtains closed after
on the summer's burglary. Flowers
seeming always to struggle. The bruised lawn.
Things loved, unloved: green hose,
snake in the grass, scabbed brick path
to the wooden shack, roofless. We kept coal
there, old buckets. Bicycle wheel?
Gardens of the damned, gardens
of unlikely pleasures, the sun meagre,
the garden furniture living in hope.
Bought in the garden centre, white
iron of Arcadia, dulling slowly. Driving
to the garden centre, suburban tropics
sweating with desire. Prams in the aisles,
the modest jungle rent with cries. Price-tags

on the foliage, the sprinklers hissing. Hands
on the leaves, tender, caressing.
Between my finger and my thumb
a feast of Latin. Everything there
lavished with its name. Such prima donnas!
Brief arias on the window sill, water
sprayed like applause. Never enough. We could never
love them enough. They thrive now
in perfect homes, brochured heavens, lifting
their juicy hearts to the sun, justly
rewarded. The lawn recovers, trimmed
by the breath of angels.

                     A voyage in July,
revving the Flymo, up, across, down,
up again in decreasing squares. Grass
in the grass-bin, falling softly.
Tartan rug, magic carpet, sprawled on it,
chewing the fringes, head dipped
in a book of places. Drooling
over the names. Zanzibar. Hindustan. Nkrumah.
Saying them to the grass. Travelling
on a wing and an ear. Failed
Geography in school, inability to associate
the right industries with the right towns.
Eindhoven. Radios, TVs. Duisburg. Radios?
TVs? Namur. Dull red-bricked town, maker
of . . . Also failed to ford the Shannon
given all the necessary information.
An *E* on the card, my life
ebbying, eddying? pouring down
to the wrong sea. All those books
for an *E* . . . . Floundering, waving apologies
towards the parental shore. Lake
Disappointment.
                   All that furniture

unbroken still, all that grass
still festering. Shovelling coal
on a winter's night, scrape, *shlock*, scrape,
shlock, the bucket bumping my leg.

Third and Fourth Ambitions

To bequeath, finally,
the white silence of myself
you would never have imagined
ached behind those words.
All that time I was rubbing
myself out. It took many volumes
to get this far. Oh how
I have had to labour
for my erasure!

To come back once more
but so lightly
nothing would mark the entrance,
not a leaf would quiver
or a single exhalation
be added to the air,
coming down in a freight of rain
with the silent messiahs
landing everywhere, wanting nothing.

Old Harvest

Almost manageable:
the sun-maddened verandah

the village on the mountain top
rocking itself to sleep

and the difficult trees
out in their far fields.
All we could do
to strip them down, taking

the barest form
                    tongues
in the dry throat of the valley
scraping the roof

remembered already, our minds
tingling down their spines
like the first rain.
Juicy mouth, a gulp of memory,

the leaves coming back again.
Wandering through
our portable farms, the first crop rising
on the back of our necks.

The Monster Remembers

Grinning like a fool, mad
half-arsed simpleton
clutching the flower, Frankenstein
ecstatic by the lake, killing the girl
out of sheer joy. Oh glad
monsters with simple hands.

The world is full.
I hold you in my hand,
my mind is empty.
Glass flower, tilting archly,
this will be the best murder.

The Show

Here we sit, mouths open, lips wet,
waiting to be astonished —
the strapless prints, the cute chemise,
the coyly, inch by inch lifted
hemline of despair . . . .

It was the era of monsters,
friendly, companionable,
above all *known*.

We lived on dark deeds,
almost, you could say,
for dark deeds. We sat in city parks
motionless but expectant.
Newspapers blundered towards us

like clumsy birds, sent from the innocent boat
and bringing back
the murderous, rat-infested
Ararat. It was the era

of eloquent nightmares.

City of Water

This city sinks carefully
into the uncomplaining mud.
Equally carefully
it is kept upright

propped by staves
and the pride of its citizens.
The streets lean over
their watery mirrors.

They shiver crookedly
and seem pleased.
My eye sinks without complaint
into the careful city.

My heart leans out
on its ribs of light.
It trembles in the water
and seems pleased.

City of Risk

There is no yearning periphery.
There are no monuments to desire.
When emotions fail they fail
quietly and without record.
The river runs unquestioned and unreflecting
through the town, careless
of what it passes or what lies on it, all
water slipping off a water's back.

As for the architecture, the lives,
how can you find words
for what doesn't stand still
long enough to need a name,
for what goes on unchecked
and unchecking? Only set down
how gently the foundations rock,
how gently also the air rushes
through the open doors.

Dinner at the Residence Hotel

Everyone has his own speed. His
might be the quick, provisional grace
he hurries through his life with,
a restless abstraction revealing itself sometimes
as the inability to stay in one place
very long, or in any one part
of whatever room he happens to be in.
Life passes through his hands
like an endless series of hot potatoes
or stolen goods, and there is always that
helpless sense of something forgotten
or lost, thrown out with the uneaten
oranges, the unidentifiable smell,
or filed in a book lent to a friend
last year somewhere. He has moved so often
that by now loss is the one constant home:
books, pictures, whole sets of crockery
abandoned on a dock or simply smashed
though there have been gains too:
a box of winter clothes opened but
untouched, left in the hall to mourn
their owner; once, a set
of misdirected encyclopaedias, *Larousse*,
which finally he mounted on his shelves.
What else? Affairs, friendships
lightly held, soft luggages of lips, whispers,
confidences flourished in the foreign night.
Knowledge of many cuisines and weathers,
his nose a library of airs, spices.
In Guatemala he had a live-in maid.
In Turkey he whistled from his window
and the minions came, bearing vegetables,
fruit, his laundry fragrant, bringing him
to dinner here with us in the complex,

five concrete towers, a thousand units
fully self-contained. We're miles from the city,
in an outlying village, though above us
huge and garish, the neon letters blurt our residence
onto the rice-fields and inside, too,
lit by wine, coffee, *amaro*,
we shine on the night as if we meant to stay.